Richard Niccols

Sir Thomas Overburies Vision

Richard Niccols

Sir Thomas Overburies Vision

ISBN/EAN: 9783337395674

Printed in Europe, USA, Canada, Australia, Japan

Cover: Foto ©Andreas Hilbeck / pixelio.de

More available books at **www.hansebooks.com**

SIR

THOMAS OVERBURIES

VISION

BY

RICHARD NICCOLS

1616

WITH INTRODUCTION BY MR. JAMES MAIDMENT.

PRIVATELY PRINTED

MDCCCLXXIII

INTRODUCTION.

HEN the valuable library of the fecond Earl of Oxford was purchafed by Thomas Ofborne, the London bookfeller, it contained a "collection of fcarce, curious, and entertaining pamphlets and tracts," many of which were confidered unique. Out of thefe was formed the "Harleian Mifcellany," which extended to eight volumes 4to, and was publifhed at London in yearly volumes, the laft of which appeared about 1747.

In the preparation of this valuable work, Ofborne had the good fortune to obtain the aid of William Oldys, Efquire, a man to whom his country is deeply indebted for many literary fervices, the merits and importance of which are better known and efteemed at the prefent date than they were in his own time. In the feventh volume of this collection will be found a reprint of "Sir Thomas Overburie's Vifion; with the Ghofts of Wefton," &c., of which Oldys gives the following abftract:*—"This is a Poem compofed in our Epic verfe, and, as may be gather'd from the feventeenth page, by the author of the additional Legends in that edition of the 'Myrror for Magiftrates,' which was printed in 4to, 1610, whofe name was Richard Niccols. It is perhaps with fome impropriety entitled 'Sir Thomas Overburie's Vifion,' for it is indeed the vifion or dream of the author, upon whofe imagination the Trial of Sir Thomas's Murderers in Guild-Hall, where he had heard it, made fuch impreffion that Sir Thomas appeared to him at night in his fleep, and led him to the Tower, and there relates how barbaroufly he was treated

* Vol. VIII., Catalogue of Pamphlets in the Harleian Library, No. 231, p. 61.

for his faithful fervices to his Mafter, (Robert Carr, Earl of Somerfet.) There is a wooden print of Sir Thomas, his Ghoft, and he concludes his tale with a requeft that our Author fhould tranfmit to pofterity his true tragedy. Then, as they are looking towards Traytor's Bridge, they fee under the Arch the Ghoft of Wefton arife out of the Thames, and he tells the Story of his Guilt in a penitential manner; and here we have his picture, with a halter about his neck. After whom appears, in the fame place, Mrs. Turner, whofe figure, in like manner alfo, is attended with her confeffion. To her fucceeds Sir Garvis Ellwis, Lieutenant of the Tower, and after him, Franklin: each in a print, attended with their fpeech. When the laft finks down, Sir Thomas winds up the whole with a Panegyrick upon the King's Juftice, in bringing his faid Murderers (except the two Noble Chiefs) to execution, and with prayers that Heaven would confound all treafonable attempts againft him and the State: Here the Author wakes, and fo ends his Vifion."

This abftract of the poem is fubftantially correct, but the verfion itfelf in the Mifcellany has the defect of modernizing the language, and omitting the woodcuts, which are fingularly interefting; and as Niccols muft have feen the unhappy fufferers during their trials, may be prefumed to poffefs fome refemblance to the criminals. The woodcut of Mrs. Turner, whofe confeffion is fo pathetically expreffed, and in which fo many beautiful paffages occur, is particularly attractive, and has been very accurately copied in the prefent reprint.

The late Charles Kirkpatrick Sharpe, Esq., had in his library a rare tract, entitled "The Juft Downfall of Ambition, Adultery, and Murder," printed at London, fmall 4to. On the title-page there is a rude cut of Mrs. Turner, of which a copy was etched by that gentleman, and prefixed, with other fimilar cuts, to the reprint of an unpublifhed work, entitled " The Whore's Rhetoric,"* originally printed, London, 12mo,

* Edinburgh, 4to, 1836.

1683. There is no refemblance whatever between the two wood engravings.

It is evident neither Anthony à Wood, nor, at a more recent period, Haflewood, ever faw a copy of the original edition of "Sir Thomas Overburies Vifion," which is of extreme rarity, and of which there is no copy in the library of the Britifh Mufeum, or in that of the Faculty of Advocates. Neither did Mr. Amos; who, in his elaborate work, entitled "The Great Oyer of Poifoning," * has quoted feveral portions of the poem, from the "Harleian Mifcellany, Vol. VII." This learned gentleman, albeit a lawyer and a member of the Supreme Council of India, duly appreciated the poetical merits of Niccols, for he ventures to fay, "The student of Englifh poetry will read with much intereft feveral of the lines; which, if he had not been apprized of their date, he would probably have fuppofed to have been written after the period of Waller and Denham."

"Richard Niccolls," fays Anthony à Wood, "efteemed eminent for his poetry in his time, was born [about the year 1584] of genteel parents in London, and at eighteen years of age, an. 1602, was entred a ftudent in Mag. coll. in Michaelmas term; but making little ftay there he retired to Mag. hall, and took the degree of bach. of arts in 1606, being then numbred among the ingenious perfons of the univerfity. After he had remained there for fome time he retired to the great City, obtained an employment fuitable to his faculty, and at length honoured the devotees to poetry with thefe things following," &c.†

Haflewood, in his reprint of the "Mirror for Magiftrates,"‡ fays that Niccols, who had publifhed an edition of that popular Mifcellany in 1610, with the text of which he had ventured to take liberties, had, when about twelve years of

---

* London, 8vo, 1846, p. 49.
† Wood's Athenæ Oxonienfes, edited by Dr. Blifs, London, 4to, 1815, Vol. II., p. 166.
‡ London, 4to, 1815, Vol. I., p. 14.

age, embarked in a veffel called the "Ark," which failed with the expedition againft Cadiz in June, 1596, and was prefent at the great and complete victory obtained by fea and land on that occafion. Whether this voyage was the refult of boyifh ardour, or that he was originally intended to be actually employed for his country in either marine or military fervice, is not known.

He appears on his return to have refumed his ftudies, and in 1602 was entered a ftudent in Magdalen College, Oxford. He took the degree of Bachelor of Arts in 1606, and was then efteemed among the "ingenious perfons of the Univerfity." In 1610 he impliedly fays he fhould have continued the "Mirror for Magiftrates" further, if his own affairs would have fuffered him to proceed, but being called away by other employments, he of force left the completion to others. What defignation thefe employments gave him for the remainder of his life, beyond that of a poet, is not known. In that character his talents would appear overrated by Headley, who confidered him "a poet of great elegance and imagination," had not Warton unwittingly gone farther. Niccols, on reprinting the "Induction," found the rhyme too perfect, and the language too polifhed, to allow the attempting of any of his fuppofed emendations, but towards the conclufion of the poem, he was bold enough to reject one ftanza, and foift in four of his own compofing; and it is to his credit that Warton, in analyfing the whole, reprinted two of thefe as the genuine production of Sackville. Such a compliment cannot be exceeded. He publifhed the "Cuckow," 4to, 1607, and he fays,

"And *Cuckow*-like of Caftaes wrongs in ruftick tunes did fing."

He reprinted the "Mirror for Magiftrates" in 1610, edited in a manner that left his volume without any value but for the adding his own poems, viz., firft, the "Fall of Princes," and laft, "A Winters Nights Vifion." This Vifion was com-

poſed probably as long before as Auguſt, 1603, as that was
the laſt calamitous year when the plague ravaged extenſively
previous to its being publiſhed. On that occaſion our author
retired for ſafety to Greenwich, where, wandering through the
walks long favoured by Elizabeth, the circumſtance of it being
her natal place, combined with her then recent death, appears
to have awakened his youthful muſe to attempt this metrical
hiſtory of her life, " Expicedium. A Funeral Oration upon the
death of the late deceaſed Princeſſe, of famous memorye,
Elizabeth," &c., 4to, 1603. He alſo wrote the "Three
Siſters Teares. Shed at the late Solemne Funerals of
the Royall deceaſed Henry, Prince of Wales," &c., 4to, 1613;
"The Fvries. With Vertves Encomium, Or the Image of
Honour. In two Bookes of Epigrammes," &c., 8vo, 1614;
" Monodia or Walthams Complaint, vpon the death of that
moſt Vertuous and Noble Ladie, late deceaſed the Lady
Honor Hay," &c., 8vo, 1615; "Londons Artillery, briefly
containing the noble praꞓife of that wo[r]thie Societie," &c.,
4to, 1616. (For an account of this poem, ſee "Britiſh
Bibliographer," Vol. I., p. 363.) "Sir Thomas Overbvries
Viſion," &c., 4to, 1616, reprinted in the " Harleian Miſcellany,"
1811, Vol. VII., p. 178. The author makes the Ghoſt of
Overbury, in his addreſs to him, ſay—

> " (*O thou mortall wight*)
> Whoſe mournefull Muſe, but whilome did recite
> Our Brittaine Princes, and their woſull ſates
> In that true (*Mirrour for our Magiſtrates.*)"

His laſt work is " The Beggers Ape," &c., 4to, 1627.

As an able bibliographer, Haſlewood deſerves great com-
mendation, but we are not prepared to aſſign much weight to
his poetical criticiſms, which ſhow that he had not drank
deeply of the Caſtalian Spring. He was a zealous follower
of the dry-as-duſt school of the period, and rather preferred
collating the different editions of the " Mirror for Magiſtrates"
than enjoying its beauties. Headley, on the other hand, whoſe

high opinion was founded exclusively upon Niccols' contributions to the "Mirror"—for he apparently had never seen the "Vision"—was a poet himself; and his "Select Beauties of Ancient English Poetry, with Remarks," published originally in 1787, when he was only twenty-two years of age, afford ample evidence of his elegant poetical taste, and his great critical ability.*

The accession of the Royal Family of Stewart to the Throne of England did not realize the anticipations of those who imagined a union of the two kingdoms would be beneficial to both. The Scots were discontented at the absence of the King and Court, whilst the English, during the entire reign of James, had but little cause for rejoicing at the presence of a Monarch who dissipated the resources of the country on his favourites, whose manners were unkingly, and whose habits were gross and sensual. His reign in England, which commenced on 24th March, 1603, and terminated on 27th March, 1625, to borrow an epithet of modern days, was throughout a sensational one.

Although James met with a hearty welcome from his new subjects, and was flattered and feasted to his heart's content, these halcyon days gradually passed away; and after two years of a deceitful calm, a combination of malcontents was forming, whose object it was to destroy the King, Lords, and Commons, by what is known as the Gunpowder Plot. His Majesty was flattered by the courtiers for the good things he scattered amongst them; but by the gentry, as well as commonality, was held in little estimation, and the contrast drawn between him and his predecessor was certainly not to his advantage. The only manly pastime of his Majesty was the chase, in which he frequently indulged, carefully guarded by a retinue of followers to protect him from harm. He had a taste for masques and pageants; patronised tilts, but seldom

---

* He died on the 15th of November, 1788, in the twenty-third year of his age.

perfonally ventured to run a courfe. To females he was cold, but an admirer of male beauty.

When he left Scotland, James took with him, as a Groom of the Chamber, a young man named Prefton, of an ancient family, neither noble nor rich, but active, handfome, and well educated. During the tournaments, fo frequently exhibited at Court, probably more for the gratification of Anne of Denmark than the delectation of her timid hufband, Prefton diftinguifhed himfelf by his agility and the fkill he difplayed in managing his fteed. He was, upon the occafion of his Majefty's coronation, 25th July, 1603, made a Knight of the Bath. Subfequently he received a Scottifh Peerage, under the title of Lord Dingwall, 8th June, 1609; and upon obtaining the hand of the Vifcountefs of Tilliophelim, the only furviving child of the Earl of Ormond, and the youthful widow of the apparent heir-male of that noble family, was created Earl of Defmond in Ireland.

Favoured as Lord Dingwall continued to be by James and his Queen, it was his fate to be eclipfed by another youth from the North, whofe fair proportion of body and beauty of countenance the Monarch found it impoffible to refift.

It is ftrange that the new favourite was brought under the notice of James by the old one. Dingwall, being ordered by the King to perform at a courtly tilting, having a regard for Robert Car or Ker, a fon of the Laird of Fernihurft—from his being, like himfelf, a native of Scotland, and from his "comely vifage" and "courtly prefence"—preferred him to carry the device to the King, according to the ufual cuftom. When he fhould have lighted from his horfe to perform his office, the animal ftarted back, threw him down, and broke his leg.* James, learning that his name was Ker, and that he was one of his pages, caufed him to be taken into the

---

* See Osborne's Traditionary Memoir in the Secret Hiftory of the Court of James I., edited by Sir Walter Scott, Edin., 8vo, 1811, Vol. I., p. 375.

Court, and attended to carefully until he recovered from his hurt. Wilfon, in his life of James, mentions that his Majefty "vifited him often during his neceffitated reftraint fometimes an hour or more, converfing with him to found him and know what he was; and though he found no great depth of literature and experience, yet fuch a fmooth and calm outfide made him think there might be a good and fit anchorage for his moft retired caufes."

In a moft amufing letter by Thomas Howard, fubfequently Earl of Suffolk, to Sir John Harrington of Kelfton,* after inftructing his friend as to his behaviour when he came to Court, he thus defcribed the ruling favourite, " Car hath all favours, as I told you before; the King teacheth him Latin every morning, and I think fome one fhould teach him Englifh too; for, as he is a Scottifh lad, he hath much need of better language. The King doth much covet his prefence; the Ladies too are not behind-hand in their admiration; for I tell you, good Knight, this fellow is ftraight-limbed, well-favourede, ftrong-fhoulderd, and fmooth-faced, with fome fort of cunning and fhow of modefty; tho', God wot, he well knoweth when to fhew his impudence." This worthy nobleman did not then imagine he was fubfequently to be a party to the unhallowed efpoufals of his profligate daughter to the " Scottifh lad."

During the period that Somerfet was thus climbing the ladder of promotion, his afcent was materially aided by Sir Thomas Overbury, whofe judicious advice and affectionate anxiety was of incalculable value to him. His counfellor was an accomplifhed gentleman, who had travelled, feen Courts, and wrote in verfe as well as profe. When at the pinnacle of power, Car threw down the ladder by which he had mounted. He had been fafcinated by the beauty and addrefs of an unprincipled female, the Lady Frances Howard, daughter of Sir

* Nichols' Progreffes of James I., London, 4to, 1828, Vol. II., p. 413.

John Harrington's correfpondent, who had been married when almoft a child to the youthful Earl of Effex—the fon of the unfortunate favourite of Queen Elizabeth.

Upon the 25th of March, 1611, Car, ftyled "fon to Thomas Car, Laird of Fernihurft," was created Vifcount Rochefter at Whitehall, with great ceremony. Upon the 21ft of April following, "Sir Thomas Overbury, having offended his friend Car, was firft imprifoned" in the Tower.*

Overbury had previoufly been the "Pythias" of "Car," and in order to influence him, his father had been made, through the Howards, a Welfh judge; the fon, "naturally of an infolent fpirit, which was elevated by being fo intimate with the favourite, and wholly having ingroffed that commodity, which could not be retayled but by him and his favor; with a kind of fcorne neglected their friendfhips, yet made ufe of both." †

Sir Anthony Weldon informs his readers that the Earls of Northampton and Suffolk, the latter his nephew, and both Howards, unable to influence Overbury as they defired, took other means of accomplifhing what they wanted by means of a "'Moabitifh woman,' a daughter of the Earle of Suffolk, married to a young noble gentleman, the Earle of Effex." This was the Lady Frances, fecond daughter of Thomas, Earl of Suffolk. Her elder fifter, Elizabeth, was the wife of William Knollys, Earl of Banbury, an aged nobleman, upon whofe death two male children were produced as born of the marriage; but their legitimacy was not allowed, and the Earldom of Banbury thereby became extinct.

A meeting was brought about at the houfe of a depraved perfon of the name of Coppinger, who, though originally of good fortune and family, had become thoroughly degraded, but was a friend of both the Howards, and a very fuitable perfon for what followed. Thefe love paffages between Car

* Nichols' Progreffes of James I., Vol. II., p. 416.
† Secret Hiftory of the Court of James I., Vol. I., pp. 376-7-8.

and Lady Frances came to the ears of Overbury, "that John Baptift that reproved the Lord for the fin of ufing the lady, and abufing the young Earl of Essex; would call her ftrumpet, her mother and brother bawds, and ufed them with fo much fcorne, as in truth was not to be endured from a fellow of his rank, to perfons of that quality, how faulty foever otherwife they were.

"Then, to fatisfie Overbury, and blot out the name of fin, his love led him into a more defperate way, by a refolution to marry another mans wife. Againft this then did Overbury bellow louder, and in it, fhewed himfelf more like an affectionate then a difcreet and moderate friend: had he compounded but one dram of difcretion with an ounce of affection, he might with fuch a receipt have preferved his own life, and their fortunes and honors." *

The firft ftep to remove Overbury was to influence the King againft him, and this was not very difficult to effect. It was arranged that he fhould be fent as Ambaffador to Ruffia. If he accepted the appointment, he was removed from all interference with the fhameful proceedings in progrefs. If he refufed, then he incurred the difpleafure of James, an act of contempt, for which he could expect nothing lefs than imprifonment. He rejected the appointment, and was committed to the Tower, which he never left alive; this imprifonment was exactly twenty-feven days after his perfidious friend had been created Vifcount of Rochefter.

Whether Damon contemplated what was to follow the incarceration of the once beloved Pythias is uncertain. That he was a party to the commitment to the Tower is plain, but at any time a fingle word to James would have procured a remiffion of the fentence. After a careful confideration of the evidence adduced on the trial of the parties implicated in Overbury's murder, there does not appear any proof that

* Secret Hiftory of the Court of James I., Vol. I., p. 379.

Somerſet was at all cogniſant of the intended murder. Of
the guilt of his wife there is not the ſhadow of a doubt. She
was the originator and prime mover, and as vindictive as
ſhe was profligate; ſhe prolonged the ſufferings of her victim
until the lateſt moment, when nature could ſuſtain the poiſonous
attack no longer, and Overbury expired—the victim of a
falacious woman.

Whilſt Overbury was in durance vile, proceedings were
inſtituted for annulling the marriage between Lady Frances
Howard and the Earl of Eſſex; and a courſe of inveſtigation
paſſed, not to be paralleled in any civilized country, in which
the King himſelf performed a prominent part. What was
done in this iniquitous affair will be found in Oſborne's
"Traditionary Memoirs," to which the reader is referred.
Abbot, Archbiſhop of Canterbury, oppoſed the whole proceedings, and proteſted againſt them, by which he incurred
the Royal diſpleaſure, "and dyed in the diſgrace of the king
on earth, though in favour with the king of kings."

Sir Thomas Overbury died on the 15th of September, 1613,
and was buried in the Tower about the ſame time the marriage
of the Earl of Eſſex and Lady Frances was pronounced a
nullity. "The morning that the matter was to be decided,
the King ſent an expreſs commandment [to the judges] that in
opening they ſhould not argue nor uſe any reaſon, but only
give their aſſent or diſſent." In the ſentence all that is ſaid is
that the marriage was null,* *propter latens et incurabile impedimentum.*†

On the 26th December following, this unhappy marriage
was conſummated, for which the "family of Suffolk paid dear
in aftertime, and had ſower ſawce to that ſweet meat of their
great ſon-in-law."‡ The writer continues, "Surely he was the

* Nichols' Progreſſes of James I., Vol. II., p. 678. The vote was ſeven for the
divorce, and five againſt it.
† Notwithſtanding this "impedimentum," Lord Eſſex married Elizabeth,
daughter of Sir William Paulet, by whom he had a ſon, Robert, who died young.
‡ Secret Hiſtory of the Court of James I., Vol. I., p. 390.

moſt unfortunate man in that marriage, being as generally beloved for himſelfe and diſpoſition, as hated afterwards for his linking himſelfe in that family; for in all the time of this mans favor, before this marriage, he did nothing obnoxious to the ſtate, or any baſe thing for his private gain; but whether it was his own nature that curbed him, or that there was then a brave prince living, and a noble queene that did awe him, we cannot ſo eaſily judge, becauſe, after this marriage and their death, he did many ill things."

Whilſt Overbury, a cloſe priſoner in the Tower, was gradually ſinking under the poiſons adminiſtered to him from day to day by the agents of the future Counteſs of Somerſet, his murderer was taking meaſures to diſſolve her marriage with the Earl of Eſſex. The King, ſtill infatuated with his favourite, and influenced by the lady's father, Suffolk, and her grand-uncle Northampton, gave his countenance to the ſtep. With his authority, and probably acting under his advice—for James prided himſelf on his legal knowledge*—a jury of matrons was ſummoned for preliminary inveſtigation; and the lady, judging it preferable to appear by proxy, induced a young female about her own figure, and attired in one of her dreſſes, to take her place, cloſely veiled, no doubt to hide her bluſhes. The perſonation ſucceeded admirably; the matrons and their venerable eccleſiaſtical and legal aſſeſſors preſent for the occaſion concurred in opinion, and declared her to be " Virgo intacta." It was preſumed this deciſion would have negatived the *fama clamoſa* which had previouſly damaged the character of this high-born lady. But although it ſatisfied Royalty, and afforded ground for the proceedings which ſpeedily followed, the public was not ſatisfied, ridiculed all the actors

* In the " Miſcellany of the Abbotsford Club," Vol. I., p. 195, there is a remarkable proof of this, being no leſs than a learned award or decreet arbitral, prepared by the King as to the ſucceſſion to the Barony of Sanquhar, the original of which is corrected throughout in his well-known handwriting. It is a very elaborate and able document. The original MS. is in the library of the Faculty of Advocates.

in this difgufting drama, and applied to the principal performer
the coarfeft epithets.*

On the 26th of December, 1613, the bridegroom, having
been previoufly created Earl of Somerfet, became hufband of
Lady Frances Howard. "The Dean of the Chapel coupled
them; which fell out ftrangely that the fame man fhould marry
the fame perfon in the fame place, upon the felf-fame day (after
eight years), the former party yet living. All the difference
was, that the King gave her the laft time, and now her father.
The King and Queen were both prefent, and tafted wafers and
ypocrafs as at ordinary weddings." The Dean of the Chapel
was Dr. Montague, Bifhop of Bath and Wells.†

Gifford, who has printed the mafque performed upon
occafion of the marriage of the Earl of Effex and the Lady
Frances Howard in 1606, in his valuable edition of the works
of Ben Jonfon,‡ compliments him for not proftituting his mufe
upon occafion of the new efpoufals of Lady Frances by any
production in honour of thefe infamous nuptials. For this
ftrange error he has been juftly taken to tafk by Nichols,
who, in the valuable work juft referred to, is furprifed
"that Mr. Gifford fhould congratulate himfelf and his readers
that Jonfon was *not* employed at all in the celebration of
the prefent ill-omened Marriage." Now, it is proved beyond
doubt that he was *doubly* employed, both in "The Challenge at
Tilt at a Marriage," 1613, and in the "Irifh Mafque." As both
thefe are printed by Gifford, it muft be prefumed he never
read either the one or the other, for the *internal* evidence
proves at once for what marriage they were intended.§

What was there wonderful in Jonfon, like other poets of the
day, who even in our times are not overburdened with riches,
taking money for placing his poetical fervices at the pleafure

* The young lady's name, as given by Sir Anthony Weldon, was Fines—
probably Fiennes.—Secret Hiftory of the Court of James I., Vol. I., p. 389.
† Nichols' Progreffes of James I., Vol. II., p. 725.
‡ London, 8vo, 1816, Vol. VII., p. 46.
§ See Appendix.

of the King on an occafion which afforded royalty much gratification. At this time the murder of Overbury had not come to light, and Somerfet, backed by the Howards, was in the afcendant. The Countefs, notwithftanding her damaged reputation, was the queen of beauty, and worfhipped at Court. Could it be imagined that Jonfon would alone refufe to contribute to the general amufement, becaufe of the very extraordinary and unheard of, but legal, procedure which had diffolved her previous matrimonial vow? Would James have overlooked and forgiven a refufal on the part of his Poet-Laureate?

Somerfet, believing his influence over the King would be perpetual, gradually loft his popularity; and the Howards, who propofed through his means to rule, became difgufted when they found how little he was inclined to benefit them. His haughtinefs and prefumption offended Anne of Denmark, and irritated her hufband, whilft the courtiers who hated the Scottifh parvenu formed a party for his deftruction.

With this intention, they felected a young man of the name of Villiers, whofe perfonal beauty it was expected would attract the notice of James. Nor were they difappointed in their anticipations. Before proceeding to open hoftilities, Villiers offered himfelf as a fuppliant, and folicited the patronage of the favourite, who rejected his offer of fervice with fcorn. War was the confequence, and the downfall of Somerfet followed. The fallen favourite fhould have remembered how he had fupplanted Dingwall, who, feeing his reign was paft, prudently refigned what he had no power to retain, and by fo doing preferved the favour of the King. It was Somerfet's attempt to oppofe the pleafure of the Monarch that brought to light the murder of Overbury, which probably otherwife might have been entirely overlooked.

As the facts are fully detailed in the State Trials, as well as in the "Great Oyer of Poifoning," which we have already noticed, it appears unneceffary to do more than refer to thefe works for fuch further information as may be required on the fubject of this moft horrible murder, its difcovery and the proceedings adopted to bring all implicated in it to trial, and the punifhment of the murderers.   The Countefs pleaded guilty; but her hufband, who was tried after her, pointedly denied his guilt, and affuredly, if the trial had taken place in Scotland, where the English diflike of the Scots would not have had any effect, the verdict could only have been one of " Not proven."

Of the inferior culprits, the only one who fuffered unjuftly was Sir Gervaife Elwes, who met with fcrimp juftice, as there was no evidence to fhew his knowledge of the adminiftration of poifoned food.   He was a man held in general eftimation, and had in thofe evil times, what was not very common, a reputation free from ftain.

Irrefpective of the great poetical merits of "Sir Thomas Overburies Vifion," it derives peculiar intereft from affording a contemporaneous defcription, accompanied by portraitures, of the unhappy perfons who were brought to the fcaffold for acting as agents of the Countefs in her atrocious and vindictive proceedings.

Wefton was brought to trial upon the 19th October, 1615, and, being found guilty, was afterwards executed.   Mrs. Turner was tried and convicted on the 7th November, 1615, when the Lord Chief Juftice Coke, the celebrated commentator on Littleton, before the jury retired to confider their verdict, told the unhappy woman that "fhe had the feven deadly fins, viz., a whore, a bawd, a forcerer, a witch, a papift, a felon, a murderer, the daughter of the Devil Forman; wifhing her to repent, and become a Servant of Jefus Chrift, and to pray to him to caft out of her thofe feven Devils." On the 14th November following, fhe was executed.   Sir Gervaife Elwes was brought to trial on the 16th November, and convicted; and Franklin was in like manner convicted on the 27th November following, and both thereafter executed.

Of the treatment of the prifoners by the Court, a fpecimen has been given in the cafe of Mrs. Turner, from which it may be inferred that her partners in guilt were dealt with in a fimilar manner. Againft Elwes there was no *legal* evidence of acceffion, and to a gentleman of birth, education, and good character, the infults offered to him muft have been even worfe than the fentence of death, afterwards pronounced upon him. "Poor Mrs. Turner," as Weldon defignates her,[*] "Wefton, and Franklyn began the tragedy, Mrs. Turners day of mourning being better than the day of her birth, for fhe dyed very penitently, and fhewed much modefty in her laft act, which is to be hoped was accepted with God. After that dyed Wefton, and then was Franklyn arraigned, who confeffed that Overbury was fmothered to death, not poyfoned to death, though he had poyfon given him."

This account of the laft moments of Anne Turner is quite in unifon with the beautiful verfes of Niccols, in which the unhappy woman, by the penitential confeffion of her fins, and her fincere contrition, appeals to the fympathy of her auditors.[†]

Somerfet and his wife were brought to trial in 1616. She was tried on the 24th of May, and was convicted upon her own confeffion. Her hufband next day boldly afferted his innocence, neverthelefs was found guilty by a jury compofed of men who had previoufly made up their minds to convict him.

The "Vifion" is dated in 1616, but has neither the name of the printer nor publifher. Nor is the place of fale given. As it fays nothing about the conviction of the two principal culprits, it may be affumed that it was compofed and circulated in the interval between the execution of Franklyn and the trial of the Countefs. It is conjectured to have not been printed for fale, Niccols being by no means certain what ufe my

* Secret Hiftory of the Court of James I., Vol. I., p. 416.
† Amos, p. 223.

Lord Chief Juftice Coke, "the very quinteffence of law," as Weldon farcaftically calls him, might have made of it. This may explain its extreme rarity.

The portraits may be affumed to bear fome refemblance to the parties intended to be reprefented, as Niccols was not a perfon, from his pofition, likely to palm any fictitious heads upon his readers, many of whom muft have been familiar with their features.

The Countefs did not follow her victims to the fcaffold, but received a pardon, which was no act of mercy, for, parted for ever from her hufband, fhe lived and died in a ftate of the greateft wretchednefs and mifery, excluded from all inter-courfe with the world, and debarred accefs to her only child, born whilft confined in the Tower, and named Anne after the Queen. Amongft the Domeftic Papers in the State Paper Office, November 17, 1615, there is preferved this interefting notice,* figned "W. Smithe:"—"The Countefs of Somerfet laying her hand on her belly faid, if I were rid of this burden, it is my death that is looked for, and my death they fhall have." The child was taken from her, and brought up in the paths of virtue. Her mother died whilft fhe was young, and every care was taken to prevent knowledge of her crimes reaching her daughter's ears. Neither was fhe allowed to breathe the foul atmofphere of the Court, until it received purification after the acceffion of Charles I., who, with all his faults, gave no countenance to vice and irreligion.

The Mafques, fo popular in the reign of Elizabeth and James, were equally fo in the reign of Charles, whofe Queen, Henrietta, not only occafionally took part in them herfelf, but induced her hufband to do fo alfo. In the year 1634, "The Temple of Love," by Inigo Jones and William Davenant, was performed by the Queen's Majefty and her Ladies at Whitehall on Shrove Tuefday. Amongft the latter was Lady

* Amos, p. 28.

Anne Carr, then about nineteen years of age. Her future hufband, Lord Ruffel, was one of the noble " Perfian Youths " prefent on this occafion; and it may be furmifed that it was during this performance the graces of the lady originated that affeftion which, three years afterwards, brought about her marriage with William, Lord Ruffel, created Duke of Bedford after the Revolution, and who died in the eighty-feventh year of his age, on the 7th of September, 1700.

" Fathers have flinty hearts," it is faid, and Francis, fourth Earl of Bedford, was no exception to the adage. Neither the charms, nor, what were preferable, the virtues of the lady, could efface the guilt of her mother, or induce the noble Earl to confent to the nuptials, though urged to do fo by the King and Queen. Plutus did what royalty could not. The Earl of Somerfet, to his credit be it fpoken, facrificed the remains of his fortune, which feems to have been greater than is ufually fuppofed, and the lovers were made happy by a payment to the Earl of £12,000, a very large fum in thofe days.

The eldeft fon of this marriage is hiftorically known as William, Lord Ruffel, who unjuftly fuffered in 1683 for his alleged participation in what is called the Rye Houfe Plot. His defcendant, the Duke of Bedford, is thus the lineal heir and reprefentative of the Earl and Countefs of Somerfet.

Somerfet was entitled to the pardon he received from the Monarch by whom he was once fo much beloved—for there was no legal evidence whatever of his participation in the guilty practices of the Countefs. If he had followed the example fhown him by his original patron, Lord Dingwall, in his own cafe, and quietly allowed George Villiers to take his place in the King's affeftion, the murder of Overbury would never have been brought to light.

The prefent reprint is a facfimile—page for page, and line for line—of the original, in the poffeffion of Mr. Alexander Young, of Glafgow.

J. M.

EDINBURGH.

APPENDIX.

THE following Lines and Note are taken from Mr. Henry Huth's "INEDITED POETICAL MISCELLANIES, 1584-1700" (printed for private circulation, 8vo, 1870):—

[UPON THE MARRIAGE OF ROBERT CAR, EARL OF SOMERSET AND FRANCES, COUNTESS OF ESSEX.[1]]

TO THE MOST NOBLE, AND ABOVE HIS TITLES, ROBERT, EARLE OF SOMERSET.

They are not thofe, are prefent wᵗh theyʳ face,
And clothes, & guifts, that only do thee grace
At thefe thy nuptials; but whofe heart and thought
Do wayte vpon thee, and theyʳ love not bought.
Such weare true wedding robes and are true Freindes,
That bid, God giue thee ioy, and haue no endes.
Wᶜh I do, early, vertuous Somerfet,
And pray thy ioyes as lafting bee as great.
Not only this, but euery day of thine,
Wᵗh the fame looke or wᵗh a better fhine.
May fhe whome thou for fpoufe to day doft take,
Out-bee yᵗ Wife in worth thy freind did make:
And thou to her, that Hufband, may exalt
Hymens amends to make it worth his fault.

[1] Believed to be unpublifhed: nor can the reafon for their fuppreffion be otherwife than obvious. Thefe lines were feemingly written, in Jonfon's familiar autograph, on the original flyleaf of a copy of one of the folio editions of his *Workes*, publifhed in 1616, and have been fubfequently pafted on to the modern fly-leaf of a copy of the folio of 1640. At the top of the page, in a different but probably coeval hand, occurs this memorandum: 'Thefe verfes were made by the

Appendix.

So be there never difcontent or forrow
To rife w^{t}h eyther of you on the morrow.
So be yor Concord ftill as deepe as mute;
And cue'ry ioy in mariage turne a fruite.
So may thofe Marriage-Pledges comforts proue:
And cu'ery birth encreafe the heate of Loue.
So in they^r number may [you] never fee
Mortality, till you [im]mortall bee.
And when your yeares rife more then would be told,
Yet neyther of.you feeme to th' other old.
That all y^t view you then, and late, may fay,
Sure this glad payre were marrie'd but this day.

BEN: JONSON.

auclhor of this booke, and were deliuered to the Earle of Somerfett vpon his Lo: wedding day: they are written by his owne hand.' * * * * The tone which the prefent lines breathe is one certainly of extravagant, but we are fcarcely, perhaps, warranted in adding *hypocritical*, laudation. Singularly enough, at a later period, when the fortunes of Car, as well as his fame, had fuffered an irrecoverable fall, a fellow-countryman, Robert Farley, dedicated to him with the moft difinterefted devotion a little book of emblems.[1] The copy of Jonfon's *Works*, 1640, from which the prefent inedited lines have been derived, is in the Britifl Mufeum, for which it was purchafed feveral years ago at Sotheby's auction-rooms.

[1] [This rare volume is entitled "KALENDARIVM HVMANÆ VITÆ THE KALENDER OF MANS LIFE. *Authore Roberto Farlæo, Scoto Britanio.* LONDON *Printed for William Hope, and are to be fould at ye vnicorne neare the Royall Exchange.* 1638." 8vo. The dedication to Somerfet is in Latin. Mr. Maidment is in poffeffion of a prefentation by the Faculty of Advocates and Writers to the Signet to a burfary in their gift for the education of indigent fcholars in the Univerfity of Edinburgh, dated 27th February, 1622, from which it appears that Robert Fairlie fone lawfull to umquhile Robert Fairlie, Goldfmith, burgh of Edinburgh, fucceeded Alexander Steven the laft poffeffor who had "paffed his cours of philofophie." The document has twenty-nine fignatures.]

Sir
THOMAS OVERBVRIES
Vision.

With the ghoasts of *Weston*, *M^{cis}. Turner*, the late *Lieftenant* of the Tower, and *Franklin.*

By *R. N. Oxon.*

--- *In pœnam infectatur & vmbra.*

PRINTED FOR *R. M. & T. I.* 1616.

SIR Thomas Overbvries
Vision.

WHen poyfon (O that poyfon and foule wrong,
     Should euer be the fubiect of my fong!)
Had fet loud Fame vpon a loftie wing,
Throughout our ftreetes with horrid voice to fing
Thofe vncouth tidings, in each itching eare,
How raging luft of late, too foone did beare
That monfter murther, who once brought to light,
Did flay the man whofe vifion I recite:
Then did th' inconftant vulgar day by day,
Like feathers in the wind, blowne euery way,
Frequent the ᵃ *Forum*, where in thickeft throng,   ᵃ Guildhall.
I one amongft the reft did paffe along
To heare the iudgement of the wife, and know
That late blacke deede, the caufe of mickle woe:
But from the reach of voice too farre compel'd,
That beaft of many heads I there beheld,
And did obferue how euerie common drudge,

          A 3   Affum'd

Aſſum'd the perſon of an awefull Iudge:

Here in the hall amidſt the throng one ſtands

Nodding his head, and acting with his hands,

Diſcourſing how the poyſons ſwift or ſlow

Did worke, as if their nature he did knowe:

An other here, preſuming to outſtrippe

The reſt in founder iudgement, on his lippe

His finger layes, and winketh with one eye,

As if ſome deeper plot he could deſcrie:

Here foure or fiue, that with the vulgar ſort

Will not impart their matters of import,

Withdraw and whiſper, as if they alone

Talk't things that muſt not vulgarly be knowne;

And yet they talke of naught from morne till noone

But wonders, and the fellowe in the moone:

Here ſome excuſe that which was moſt amiſſe;

Others doe there accuſe, where no crime is,

Accuſing that which they excuſ'd anon,

Inconſtant people, neuer conſtant known:

Cenſure from lippe to lippe did freely flie,

He that knew nothing, with the reſt would crie,

The voice of iudgement; euery age ſhall finde

        Th' igno-

Th' ignoble vulgar cruell, mad in minde:

The muddie fpawne of euery fruitleffe braine,

Daub'd out in ignominious lines, did ftaine

Papers in each mans hand, with rayling rimes

Gainft the foule Actors of thefe wel-knowne crimes:

Bafe wittes, like barking curres, to bite at them

Whom iuftice vnto death fhall once condem.

I that beheld, how whifpering rumour fed

The hungrie eares of euery vulgar head

With her ambiguous voyce; night being come,

Did leaue the *Forum* and returned home;

Where after fome repaft, with greife oppreft

Of thefe bad dayes, I tooke me to my reft:

And in that filent time, when fullen night

Did hide heau'ns twinckling tapers from our fight,

And on the earth with blackeft lookes did lowre,

When euery clocke chimb'd twelue, the midnight houre,

In which imprifon'd ghoafts free licence haue

About the world to wander from their graue;

When hungrie wolues and wakefull dogges do howle

At euery breach of aire, when the fad owle

On the houfe top beating her balefull wings,

A defcription of midnight.

And

Sir Thomas

And fhreeking out her dolefull ditty, fings
The fong of death, vnto the ficke that lie
Hopeleffe of health, forewarning them to die:
Iuft at that houre, I thought my chamber dore
Did foftly open, and vpon the floare
I heard one glide along, who at the laft
Did call and bid me wake; at which agaft
I vp did looke, and loe, a naked man
Of comely fhape, but deadly pale and wan.

Sir *Thomas Ouer-*
buries ghoaft.

Before

Before me did appeare, in whoſe ſad looke,
As in the mappe of griefe or ſorrowes booke,
My eye did reade ſuch characters of woe,
As neither paintings, skill, nor pen can ſhowe:
With dreadfull horrour almoſt ſtricken dead
At ſuch a ſight, I ſhrunke into my bed,
But the poore Ghoaſt to let me vnderſtand
For what he came, did waft me with his hand,
And ſorrowes teares diſtilling from his eies,
His poyſon'd limbs he ſhow'd, and bad me riſe,
Which fearefull I, not daring diſobey,
Roſe vp and follow'd, while he lead the way
Through many vncouth wayes, he led me on
Ouer that Towers fatall hill, whereon
That ſcaffold ſtands, which ſithence it hath ſtood
Hath often lickt vp treaſons taynted blood:
Thence ouer that ſame wharfe, faſt by whoſe ſhoares
From Londons bridge the prince of riuers roares,
He in a moments ſpace by wondrous power,
Tranſported me into that ſpacious Tower,
Where as we entred in, the very ſight
Of that vaſt building, did my ſoule affright:

There did I call to minde, how or'e that gate,

The chamber was, where vnremorfefull fate

[b] *Edwards*,and his brother the Duke of York. Did worke the falls of thofe two [b]Princes dead,

Who by their foes were fmothered in their bed.

And there I did behold that fatall greene,

Where famous *Eſſex* woefull fall was feene:

Where guiltie *Suffolks* guiltleffe daughter *Iane*

The fcaffold with her noble blood did ftaine:

Where royall *Anne* her life to death refign'd,

[c] Queene *Eliza-beth*. Whofe wombe did beare the [c]praife of women kind:

[d] *Margaret* Coū-teſs of Saliſ-bury, daughter of the Duke of Clarence. And where the laft [d]*Plantaginet* did pore

Her life out in her blood, where many more,

Whom law did iuftly, or vniuftly taxe,

Paſt by the fentence of the bloody axe:

And here as one with fuddaine forrow ftroke,

The Ghoaft ftood ftill a while, with dolefull looke

Fixt on the ground, and after fad fighes giuen

With eyes and hands vp-lifted vnto heauen,

As calling them to witneffe of his woe,

In fad complaint, his griefe he thus did fhow.

    Great God of heauen, that pittieft humane wrongs,

To whom alone reuenge of blood belongs;

                          Thou

Thou, that vpon the wings of heauen do'ſt ride,

And laugh'ſt to ſcorne the man, that ſeekes to hide

And *ouer-burie* guiltleſſe blood in duſt,

Thou know'ſt the paines of my impoyſon'd ghoaſt;

When men more changing then th' inconſtant winde,

Or doe not know, or knowing wilfull blinde,

Will not behold dead *Ouerburies* griefe,

But thinke his loſſe no more then loſſe of life:

(Ye friends vnkind and falſe) that after death

Doe let your friendſhip vaniſh with the breath

Of him that's dead, and thinke ſince truth begun

To trie my cauſe, more ſatisfaction done

Then all my wrongs require; giue eare, and ſay

When I haue told my griefe, if from the day

That mans firſt blood to heauen cri'd out of earth,

For vengeance 'gainſt the firſt mans eldeſt birth

Vntill this time; if man for life ſo loſt,

More iuſtly may complaine, then my dead ghoaſt.

I was (aye me, that I was euer ſo)

Belou'd in court, firſt ſtep to all my woe:

There did I gaine the grace of Prince and Peeres,

Knowne old in iudgement, though but young in yeers;

And there, as in this Kingdomes garden, where
Both weedes and flowers doe grow, my plant did beare
The buddes of hope, which flowring in their prime
And *May* of youth, did promife fruit in time:
But luft, foule luft did with a hand of blood
Supplant my plant, and crop me in the budde:
Yet to my felfe had I my counfells kept,
Or had I drown'd my cares in reft, and flept,
When I did breake my quiet fleepes, and waite
To ferue a falfe friend, and aduance his ftate,
I had not met with this inhumane wrong,
But might perhaps haue happy liu'd, and long.
Did euer fortune pinch him with conftraint?
That little wealth I had, fupply'd his want:
Did euer cares perplex his feeble braine?
What wit I had, his weakeneffe did fuftaine:
Did euer error make him doe amiffe?
What wifedome I had learn'd, was euer his:
My wit, my wealth, and wifedome with good chaunce,
In his great honours May-game, lead the daunce.
I doe not falfly boaft the gifts of mind,
Beft wittes can iudge, my *Wife* I left behind

Vnto

Vnto the world, a witneſſe may remaine,

I had no dull conceit, no barren braine:

But as a dogge that at his pray doth ame,

Doth onely loue the water for his game,

Which once obtain'd, he playing then no more,

Shakes off the water when he comes on ſhore:

So my great Friend, no friend, but my great Foe,

Safe ſwimming in that way which I did ſhowe,

Through dangers waters after honours game,

Did ſhake me off when I had gain'd the fame.

Vaine man, too late thou do'ſt repent my wrong,

That huge great ſayle of Honour was too ſtrong

For thy great boate, wanting thy friend to ſteare:

In this, thy weakeneſſe and my worth appeare:

O hadſt thou kept the path by me begunne,

That other impious race thou hadſt not runne:

In wayes of vice thy ſteps I did not guide,

Onely for vertue *Ouerburie* di'd:

But had ingratitude no further gone,

I had not wail'd with many a piteous grone

Theſe poyſoned limbes; O how will future times

Bluſhing to heare ſuch execrable crimes

Beleeue

Beleeue report, when then it fhall be faid,

Thou waft that man, that man that me betray'd,

That fauage man, that wanting meanes or heart,

Or rather both to meete with my defert,

Too cruell didft deuife to ftop my breath,

To end thy care, and my deare life by death :

Death, oh no death, but thoufand deathes in one,

For had it bin but meere priuation

Of loued life, my greiued Ghoaft had fled

Without fuch paine and anguifh to the dead :

O wretched foes! why did yee take delight

To excercife your hate with fuch defpight

Vpon a guiltleffe man? what had I done?

But that yee might, when as ye firft begunne

Your tragicke plot, and did my life awaite,

With fingle death haue fatisfied your hate?

Was it, ah was it not enough to giue

One poyfon firft, and then to let me liue?

Till ye did pleafe to giue an other, then,

An other, and an other; but as men,

All made of flint, to laugh my plaints to fcorne,

And fcoffe at me, while I alas did mourne :

When

When in my chamber walls, the very ftones
Sweat droppes for teares to heare my greiuous grones;
As fenceleffe, they would fimpathize my woes,
Though my fad cries were muficke to my foes.
Let ages paft vntill the worlds firft day,
Shew all records of antique times, and fay
If euer any did by poyfon die,
That at his death had greater wrong then I.
It was not one dayes fpace, nor two, nor three,
In which thofe cruell men tormented me:
Month after month, they often did inftill
The diuers natures of that banefull ill
Throughout thefe limbs; inducing me to thinke,
That what I tooke in Phyficke, meate, or drinke,
Was to reftore me to my health; when all
Was but with lingring death to worke my fall.
Oh how my Ghoaft doth quake, when it furuayes
This fatall houfe, where I did end my daies!
And trembles, as it fuffered now againe,
Onely to thinke vpon that woefull paine;
When the flow poyfon fecretly did creepe
Through all my veines, and as it went, did fweepe

All

All eafe with paine, all reft with griefe away,
From euery corner of my houfe of clay:
Then did I loath my life, but could not die,
Sometimes to God, fometimes to men I crie
To giue me eafe of my tormenting hell,
Whofe paine no pen can write, no tongue can tell:
In vaine my tongue thou vtterd'ft forth my cries
To wicked men, with teare-tormented eyes;
In vaine mine eies in you the teares did ftand,
While I to heauen for helpe did lift my hand;
In vaine my hands were ye ftretcht forth to heauen,
My time was fet, my life to death was giuen:
Tongue, eyes, and hands did often plead in vaine,
Nothing but death could eafe me of my paine:
And death at laft to my defire did yeeld,
Who with fuch furious force did take the field
T'affayle my foule, that 'gainft his matchleffe might,
In greater torment neuer man did fight;
With poifon'd dart he at my life did ftrike,
The venome feazing on me vulture-like,
With torment tore my entrayles; thence did runne
Into my vaines, and boyling there begunne

A frefh

A frefh affault, which beeing a while withftood

By natures force, at laft did feaze my blood:

Then victor-like, poffeft of euery part,

It did affaile my yet not yeelding heart,

The foules cheife feate, where hauing vanquifht all

The powers of life, while I to God did call

For grace and mercy , after fad fighs giuen

With greiuous grones, my foule fled hence to heauen.

O thou fad monument of *Norman* yoke,

Whofe great foundation hee , whofe conquering ftroke

Did ftoope our neckes to *Norman* rule ᵉfirft laid,

Looke thy records of thofe, to death betray'd

Within thy fatall chambers, and there fee

If any murdered, loft his life like mee.

Thofe royall rofes of *Plantagineft,*

Which that white boare of ᶠYorke, that bloody beaft

Hath rooted vp, within thofe walls of thine,

In death felt little paine compar'd to mine:

Thou knoweft that ᵍKing, fon to that kingly Knight,

Beneath whofe fword in *Agincourts* great fight,

France fell vpon her knees, thy flore did ftaine

With his deare blood, by bloody *Richard* flaine:

e Out of a regifter booke of the acts of the Bifhop of Rochefterin*Stowes* furuay.

f *Richard* the third.

g*Henry*the fixt.

Sir Thomas

Thou didſt looke on, when *Clarence* blood was ſhed,

And didſt behold, how hee poore Duke halfe dead,

Yet bleeding freſh, in Malmeſie-but was dround,

Whoſe body ſithence neuer could be found:

Thou ſawſt when ʰ *Tirrels* bloody ſlaues did ſmother

This kingdomes vncrownd King, and his young brother

Thoſe princely babes of Yorke, thou heardſt them crie,

When they betwixt the ſheets did ſtrangled die;

But to their paine death did ſwift end aſſigne,

Thou know'ſt their greifes were not ſo great as mine.

T'was not for naught, that thy firſt builders hand

Did temper ⁱblood with burned lime and ſand,

So to conglutinate thy ſtony maſſe,

And bring the Conquerours will and worke to paſſe:

Well may it be, thy walls with blood were built,

Where ſo much guiltleſſe blood hath ſince bin ſpilt.

But here an end of all my paine and woe,

Death ſhuts vp all our greateſt greifes, for ſo

All men would thinke; but paſt all thought of minde,

My greateſt greife, alas, is yet behind.

Oh why ſhould fierceſt beaſt of all the wood,

When hee hath ſlaine his foe, and lickt his blood,

Enc

End hate in death, and man with man in ftrife,

Not end his malice with the ende of life?

Can they be men and lords of beafts, that beare

Their Makers image, and will yet not feare

That ill, which beafts abhorre in brutifh minde?

Men, O no men, but monfters againft kind:

Such monfters were my tyger-hearted foes,

Who vnremorfefull of my forepaft woes,

When from their cruell hands my foule was fled,

Did with their tongues purfue me beeing dead;

And yet not dead, for heauen fuch grace doth giue,

My foule in heauen, my name on earth doth liue:

My name, as great *Apollo's* flowring bay

Lookes greene when winter clads the earth in gray,

Did flourifh, blowne vpon by fames faire breath,

In euery eye, long time before my death;

When my proud foes of great and glorious name,

Were blafted by the breath of foule defame:

At good report, that on her golden wings

Did beare my name, their tongue like adder-ftings

Did fhoot foule flanders poyfon, fo to fpill

The fame with foule defame, as they did kill

My body with foule death, that men might loath
My liuing name, and my dead body both,
Falfe rumour, that mad monfter, who ftill beares
More tongues about with her, then men haue eares,
With fcandall they did arme, and fent her out
Into the world, to fpread thofe lies about;
That thofe loath'd fpots, marks of their poyfning finne,
Which di'd with vgly marble, paint the skinne
Of my dead body, were the marks moft iuft
Of angry heau'ns fierce wrath for my foule luft:
O barbarous cruelty! oh more then fhame
Of fhameleffe foes! with luft to blaft my name,
When wonder t'was, heauens iudgement did not feaze
Their wanton bodies, with that great difeafe,
Since death to me by poyfon they did giue,
That they in am'rous iolity might liue.
Now when falfe rumours breath throughout the court
And citty both, had blowne this falfe report,
Many, that oft before approu'd my name
With praife for vertue, blufht, as if the fhame
Of my fuppofed vice, thus giuen forth,
Did argue their weake iudgement of my worth:

                                              My

My friends look't pale with anger, and my foes

Did laugh, to ſee too light beleefe cauſe thoſe

That lou'd me once, to loath that little duſt

I left behind me, as a lumpe of luſt.

O moſt inhumane wrong! O endleſſe greefe!

O ſad redreſſe! where ſorrowes beſt releefe

Is but dead hope, that helpe may chance be found

With thoſe that liue, to cure my credits wound:

For this, my reſtleſſe ghoaſt hath left the graue,

And ſtole through couert ſhades of night, to craue

Thy pens aſſiſtance, (*O thou mortall wight*)

Whoſe mournefull Muſe, but whilome did recite

Our Brittaine Princes, and their wofull ſates

In that true *(Mirrour for our Magiſtrates.)*

O let thy pen paint out my tragicke woe,

That by thy Muſe all future times may know

My ſtories truth, who hearing thy ſad ſong,

At leaſt, may pitty *Ouerburies* wrong.

This ſaid, the grieued ghoaſt with ſighs did ceaſe

His rufull plaints, and as in deepe diſtreſſe,

Vnder the *Towersgate* with me he ſtood,

This accident befell on *Thames* great flood.

South by this houfe, where on the wharfe faſt by

Thoſe thundering Canons euer ready lie,

A docke there is, which like a darkeſome caue

Archt ouer-head, lets in *Thames* flowing waue,

Vnder whoſe *Arch*, oft haue condemned men,

As through the *Stygian lake*, tranſported been

Into this fatall houſe, which euermore

For treaſon hoards vp torturing racks in ſtore:

At landing of this place, an yron gate

Locks vp the paſſage, and ſtill keeping ſtraite

The guilty priſoners, opens at no time

But when falſe treaſon, or ſome horrid crime

Knocks at the ſame, from whence by lawes iuſt doome,

Condemned men but ſieldome backe do come:

(What'ere thou art may chance to paſſe that way,

And view that place, vnto thy ſelfe, thus ſay ;

God keepe me faithfull to my Prince and ſtate,

That I may neuer paſſe this *yron* gate:)

There in the docke the flood that ſeem'd to gape,

Did ſuddenly giue vp a dreadfull ſhape.

                                        A man

Wettons ghoaſt.

A man of megar lookes, deuoy'd of blood.
Vpon whoſe face deaths pale complexion ſtood;
Of comely ſhape, and wel compoſ'd in limme,
But ſlender made, of viſage ſterne and grimme;
The haires vpon his head and griſly beard
With age growne hoarie, here and there appear'd;
Times iron hand with many a wrinckled fret,
The marks of age, vpon his front had ſet:

The deſcription
of *Viſion*.

Yet

Yet as it did appeare, vntimely death
For fome foule fact had ftopt his vitall breath
With that great fhame, which giues offence the checke,
The fatall rope, that hung about his necke:
Trembling vpon his knees in great affright,
When he faft by beheld the poyfned Knight,
He humbly fell, and with fad greife oppreft,
Wringing his hands, and beating on his breaft,
While forrowes droppes vpon his cheekes did run,
To vtter forth thefe words, he thus begun.

O worthy Knight, behold the wretched man,
Who thy fad Tragedies firft fceane began,
Through whofe each act, vnto this laft blacke deede,
With bloody minde, vnbleft, I did proceede:
My hands, alas, did mixe the poifned food,
Which kindled cruell fire in thy blood;
Mine eares did heare thy lamentable grones,
When the flow-working-poyfon wrackt thy bones;
Mine eies without one droppe of forrow fhed,
Beheld thee dying, and beheld thee dead;
For which both hands, eyes, eares, and euery part,
Haue fuffered death, and confcience bitter fmart.

I was

I was that inftrument, alas the while,

By thy great foes inftructed to beguile

Thy lingring hopes their mighty ftate did whet

Mee on in mifcheife, and their bounty fet

A golden edge vpon my dull confent,

At once to worke thy fall, and their content.

The doctrine of that *whoore*, that would difpence

With fubiects for the murther of a Prince,

Taught me that luft and blood were flender crimes,

And he that ferues his turne, muft ferue the times.

Oh had I neuer knowne that [k]*Doctors* houfe,

Where firft of that *whoores* cup I did caroufe,

And where difloyalty did oft conceale

Romes frighted rattes, that ouer feas did fteale;

My thoughts perhaps, had then not giuen way,

Thy life for gold with poyfon to betray.

But yee that doe, and who doe not condem

My blacke offences? when yee thinke on them,

In fuch imaginations, ponder too

What with weake man, the power of gold may doe.

Ye feruile fycophants, whofe hopes depend

On great mens wills; what is the vtmoft end

k Doct. *Tur ner.*

At which ye aime? why doe ye like bafe curres,

Vpon your Patron fawne? why like his fpurres,

Will ye be euer ready at his heeles,

With pleafing words to clawe him, where he feels

The humour itch? or why, will ye fo waite,

As to lie downe and kiffe the feete of ftate?

And oft expofe your felues to wretched ends,

Loofing your foules to make great men your friends?

Is it not wealth yee feeke? and doth not gold

Ingenuous wittes ofttimes in bondage hold?

The ftout fea-rangers on the fearefull flood,

That hunt about through *Neptunes* waterie wood,

And o're a thoufand rockes and fands, that lie

Hid in the deepe, from pole to pole doe flie;

Who often, when the ftormy Ocean raues,

Fights with fierce thunders, lightnings, winds and waues,

Hauing but one fmall inch of boord, to ftand

Betwixt them and ten thoufand deaths at hand,

Expofe themfelues to all this woe and paine,

To quench the greedy thirft of golden gaine.

O ftrong inchauntment of bewitching gold!

For this, the Syre by his owne fonne is fold,

For

For this, the vnkind brother fells the brother,

For this, one friend is often by an other

Betray'd to death; yea euen for this, the wife

Both fells her beauty, and her husbands life:

And I, ay me, for this did worke thy fall

By poyfons helpe, hauing this hope withall,

That great mens greatnes, would haue boren out

My crime, though knowne, againft all dangers doubt.

But now too late, my wretched ghoaft doth proue,

That his all-feeing eye from heauen aboue,

To whom blacke darkeneffe felfe, is far more cleare

Then the bright funne, makes guiltleffe blood appeare

Out of our deepeft plots, to murthers fhame,

Though greateft men doe feeke to hide the fame.

Ye hapleffe inftruments of mighty men;

Ye fpunges, whom the hands of greatnes, when

That they by you haue wiped out the fpot

Of that difgrace, which did their honour blot,

Do fqueeze fo long, vntill that ye be drie,

And then as needleffe things doe caft ye by:

Where one of thefe your feruice would imploy,

Our makers heauenly image to deftroy,

By

By violence of death in other men,
Thereby with blood to fatisfie his fpleen:
O do not truft the hopes of fuch a man,
Nor thinke his policie or power can
Hoodwinke all-feeing heauen, nor euer drowne
The crie of blood, which brings fwift vengeance downe.
When many men, but one mans life will fpill,
Their liues for his, heauen euermore doth will.
Offend in murder, and in murder die,
No crime to heauen, fo loud as blood doth crie.
In other wrongs, when man doth man offend,
We reftitution may in part pretend:
But where the wrong is done by murthers knife,
No price for blood the Law fayes, life for life.
The eye of wakefull iuftice, for a feafon
May feeme to winke at murthers bloody treafon;
Yet from the houre of fo blacke a deede,
The worme of confcience on the foule doth feede;
And dreadfull furies, whofe imagin'd fight
In euery place, doth horribly affright
The guilty man, purfue the fteps that flie,
While fwift-wing'd vengeance makes the hue and crie.
Iuftice to me did feeme to fleepe a while,
And with delay did all my hopes beguile;
But in fhort time now in my riper yeares,

When

When grauer age on my gray head appeares,
Death and reproach attach't my life and name,
To bring me to my graue with greater ſhame:
To you therefore that hunger after gold,
To you, whom hope of great mens grace makes bold
In any great offence, henceforth let me
For euermore a ſad enſample be.
This ſaid, he ſighing ſhrunke into the flood,
And in a moments ſpace, an other ſtood

Miſt. *Turners*
ghoſt.

In the fame place; but fuch a one whofe fight

With more compaffion moou'd the poyfned Knight:

It feem'd that fhee had been fome gentle dame,

· For on each part of her faire bodies frame,

Nature fuch delicacie did beftow,

That fairer obiect oft it doth not fhow:

Her chryftall eye beneath an yuorie brow,

Did fhew what fhee at firft had been; but now

The rofes on her louely cheekes were dead,

The earths pale colour had all ouer-fpread

Her fometimes liuely looke, and cruell death

Comming vntimely, with his wintrie breath

Blafted the fruit, which cherrie-like in fhowe

Vpon her dainty lips did whilome growe:

O how the cruell cord did mif-become

Her comely necke, and yet by Lawes iuft doome

Had been her death: thofe locks like golden thred

That wont in youth t'enfhrine her globe-like head,

Hung carelefle downe; and that delightfull limme,

Her fnow-white nimble hand, that wont to trimme

Their treffes vp, now fpitefully did teare

And rend the fame: nor did fhe now forbeare

To

To beate that breaſt of more then lilly white,

Which ſometimes was the lodge of ſweete delight:

From thoſe two ſprings where ioy did whilome dwell,

Griefes pearly droppes vpon her pale cheeks fell,

And after many ſighes, at laſt with weake

And fainting voyce, ſhee thus did ſilence breake.

   Thou gentle Knight, whoſe wrongs I now repent,

Behold a wofull wretch, that did conſent

In thy ſad death: for I, alas therefore

By gold my ſeruant did ſuborne to pore

That death into thy cup, thy diſh, thy diet,

Whoſe paine too long did rob thy ghoaſt of quiet:

Yet neither thirſt of gold, nor hate to thee

For iniuries receiu'd, incenſed me

To ſeeke thy life; but loue, deare loue to thoſe

That were my friends, and thy too deadly foes:

With them in Court my ſtate I did ſupport,

Ah, that my ſtate had neuer known the Court!

Vertue and vice I there together ſawe,

But like the ſpider, I was taught to drawe

Foule poyſon, where ſweet hony might bee had,

And how to leaue the good, and chuſe the bad:

At

At laſt, through greedy going on in ſinne
Made ſenſeleſſe, by degrees I did beginne
To riſe from great to greater, till at laſt
Mine owne ſinnes did mine owne deſtruction haſt.
O heauy doome! when heauen ſhall ſo decree,
That ſinne in man the plague of ſinne muſt bee.
But here let chaſteſt beauties when they blame
My follies moſt, and bluſh to heare my ſhame,
Remember then beſt beauties are but fraile,
And how that ſtrongeſt men do oft aſſaile
Our weakeſt ſelues; ſo may they pitty me,
And my ſad fall may their fore-warning be.
Yee tender offspring of that rib, refin'd
By Gods owne finger, and by him aſſign'd
To be a helpe, and not a hurt to man;
How is it poſſible your beauties can
Be pure from blemiſh, treading ſuch vaine wayes
As now you doe in theſe prophaner dayes?
Muſt fleſh that is ſo fraile ſtill feare to fall,
And ye the fraileſt fleſh not feare at all?
Can ye, ah can ye, with vaine thoughts to pleaſe
Your wanton ſoules, on yuorie beddes of eaſe

Spend

Spend pretious time, and yet fuppofe in this

Ye doe no ill, nor thinke one thought amiffe?

Can ye to catch the wandring thoughts of him

Whom ye affect, decke euery dainty lim,

Powder your haire, and more to pleafe the eye,

Refrefh your paler cheekes with purer die,

Lay out your breafts; and in the glaffe thus dreft,

Obferue what fmile, or frowne becomes yee beft?

And yet not feare heau'ns iudgement in the end,

At leaft in this, not thinke ye doe offend?

Can ye on wanton meates to mooue defire,

Though of your felues too full of *Paphian* fire,

Feede euery houre, and when hot blood begins

To hurrie you vnto thofe horrid finnes,

That fpots your beddes, your bodies, and your names,

Blot your blacke foules with many greater blames?

And yet not thinke, ye doe deferue heauens hate,

At leaft to turne, doe thinke no time too late?

O doe not footh your felues in thefe foule crimes,

Heare not the tongue of thefe inchanting times:

Your too much idle eafe, which opes the gate

To vitious thoughts, I know is counted ftate:

E 1   Vpon

Vpon your curious pride and vaine aray,

Fond men the name of cleanlines do lay:

Your luft whofe fparkles, in your eyes doe fhine,

On wanton youth, is called loue diuine:

Thus they that would for each foule fault excufe you,

And turne your vice to vertue, doe abufe you.

But be ye not fo blinded, looke on me,

And let my ftory in your cloffets be

As the true glaffe, which there you looke vpon,

That by my life, ye may amend your owne.

Obferue each ftep, when firft I did begin

To tread the path, that lead from fin to fin,

Vntill my moft vnhappie foote did lite,

In guiltleffe blood of this impoifned Knight:

After I had in Court begun to taft

Of idle eafe, I daily fedde fo faft

Vpon falfe pleafure, that at laft I did

Climbe *Cithardas* hill, like wanton kid

In fertile paftures playing; naught did feare me,

I thought that roaring Lyon would not teare me.

Two darling finnes, too common and too foule,

With their delights did then bewitch my foule;

Firft

First pride aray'd me in her loofe attires,

Fed my fond fancie fat with vaine defires,

Taught me each fafhion, brought me ouer-feas

Each new deuife, the humorous time to pleafe:

But of all vaine inuentions, then in vfe

When I did liue, none fuffer'd more abufe

Then that phantafticke vgly fall and ruffe,

Daub'd o're with that bafe ftarch of yellow ftuffe:

O that my words might not be counted vaine,

But that my counfell might find entertaine

With thofe, whofe foules are tainted with the itch

Of this difeafe, whom pride doth fo bewitch,

That they doe thinke it comely, not amiffe:

Then would they caft it off, and fay, it is

The baud to pride, the badge of vanity,

Whofe very fight doth murther modeflie,

Ye then detefting it, they all would knowe,

Some wicked wit did fetch it from belowe,

That here they might expreffe by this attire

The colour of thofe wheeles of Stygian fire,

Which prides plūg'd ofspring with fnake-powdred haire,

About their necks in *Plutoes* Court doe weare.

E 2   Thus

Thus pride, the pandar to luxurious thoughts,

Did guide me by the hand through thofe clofe vaults,

That lead to lufts darke chambers, darke as night,

The eyes of luft doe ne're abide the light.

But here perhaps fome curious dame, who knowes

No good, but what her outward habit fhowes,

Will iudge my true complaint, as moft vniuft,

In that I call her pride, the baud to luft:

But had her bodie windowes in each fide,

That each one might behold her heart of pride,

There might one fee the caufe, why fhe doth trimme,

Tricke vp, and decke defects in euery limme;

And hauing feene the fame, may iuftly fay,

Her loofe attire doth her loofe mind bewray.

Of this the fad effects of yore were feene

1 *Raphael Hollin-fhead* in his hiftory of Engg-land.

In Lady ᵏ*Alfrith*, fometimes Englands Queene,

Whofe Lord Earle *Ethelwald*, at firft held deare

To her affection: when that he did heare

That his great Sou'raigne, royal *Edgar*, hee

Whom eight Kings row'd vpon the riuer *Dee*,

Vnto his houfe did purpofe to repaire,

Knowing his deereft Lady wondrous faire,

And

And the King young and wanton, did defire
That fhee would lay afide her rich attire,
And choofing meaner weeds, her art apply
To dimme that beautie which did pleafe the eye:
But fhee, inconftant Lady, knowing well,
That beauty moft fet forth, doth moft excell;
As precious ftones when they are fet in gold,
Are then moft faire and glorious to behold;
Arai'd her felfe in all her proud attire,
To fet victorious Edgars heart on fire:
Who caught like filly flie into the flame,
At fuddaine fight of fuch a dainty dame,
To coole the heat of his luft-burning will,
Her wronged husbands guiltleffe blood did fpill.
With pride thus tafting of that wanton cup
Which luft did giue me, I was giuen vp
To loofe defire: which bruitifh finne, fince here
In it's owne fhape it may not well appeare,
Leaft it offend all modeft eyes and eares,
I onely doe lament with my true teares:
Yet giue me leaue, in fome few words to tell
This wanton world, into what horrid hell

Of

Of wicked finnes, foule luft did make me fall,

That vnchaft youth from luft I may recall.

As euery euill humour, which is bred

In humane bodies, couets to be fed

With that ill nutriment which doth increafe

The fame, vntill it grow to fome difeafe

Incurable; fo did my loofe defire

In vaine delights, feeke fewell for the fire

So long, vntill (aye me) vnto my fhame

It did burft forth, and burne me in the flame.

I left my God t'aske counfell of the deuill,

I knew there was no helpe from God in euill:

As they that goe on whooring vnto hell,

From thence to fetch fome charme or magicke fpell,

So ouer *Thames*, as o're th' infernall lake,

A wherrie with their oares I oft did take,

Who *Charon*-like did waft me to that *Strand*,

Where *Lambeths* towne to all well knowne doth ftand;

There *Forman* was, that fiend in humane fhape,

That by his art did act the deuills ape:

Oft there the blacke Inchanter, with fad lookes

Sate turning ouer his blafphemous bookes,

Making

Making ſtrange charaƈters in blood-red lines:

And to effeƈt his horrible deſignes,

Oft would he inuocate the fiends below,

In the ſad houſe of endleſſe paine and woe,

And threaten them, as if he could compell

Thoſe damned ſpirits to confirme his ſpell.

O prophane wretches! ye that doe forſake

Your faith, your God, and your owne ſoules, to take

Aduiſe of Sorcerers, againe to finde

Some trifle loſt; why will ye be ſo blind

On ſome baſe beldam for loſt things to fawne?

To gaine whoſe loſſe, ye leaue your ſoules in pawne.

Too many, too much wronged by the time,

Do thinke this great idolatrie no crime;

But let them marke the path which they do tread,

And they ſhall ſee, that in it they are lead

From hope and helpe, to hurt and all annoy,

From him that made, to him that doth deſtroy.

But without mercie here, let no ſterne eye

Looke on my faults; alas for charity,

Let all with pitty my offence bemone,

Since that it was not my offence alone:

The

The ftrongeft foone doe flip, as I did fall,

For woe is me, I was feduc'd to all.

Yee that deteft my now detected fhame,

And thinke that ye fhall neuer meet the fame,

Thinke how the friendfhip, and the auncient loue

Of fome great Lady long enioy'd may mooue:

And thinke with that, how much the rifing ftate

Of fome great man, my fex might animate:

I was not bafe, but borne of gentle blood,

My nature of it felfe inclin'd to good,

But wormes in faireft fruit doe fooneft breed,

Of heauenly grace beft natures haue moft neede.

Iuft heauen did fuffer me, as I begunne

To haften on from vice to vice, and runne

My felfe in finnefull race quite out of breath,

That finne at laft might punifh finne by death:

For when thofe wantons, whofe vniuft defire

Had vrg'd me on fo farre, that to retire

I knew was vaine, as I before to luft

Had beene a minifter, fo now I muft

Ioyne hands in blood, which they did plot and ftudy:

O who would thinke that women-kind were bloody!

                                        But

But when our chaftitie we doe forgoe,
That loft, what then will wee refufe to doe?
This did that Romane proud ^m Seianus know,   m *Tacitus* annals, lib. 4. c. 2.
Who hating Drufus as his deadly foe,
And bafely feeking to betray his life,
Did firft allure faire Liuia Drufa's wife
To poyfon her owne Lord, that in his ftead
The bafe Seianus might enioy his bedde;
Who raif'd by Cæfar from ignoble place,
In Liuiaes luftfull eie did finde more grace
Then Drufus, Cæfars fonne, a manly youth:
O who knowes how to feed a womans tooth!
In mifchiefe I went on, and did agree
To be an actor in thy Tragedie,
Thou iniur'd ghoaft; yet was I but a mute,
And what I did was at an others fuite:
Their plots I faw, and filent kept the fame,
For which my life did fuffer death and fhame;
For fee, ah fee, this cord about my necke,
Which time fometime with pretious things did decke,
Reuenge hath done, and Iuftice hath her due,
Let none then wrong the dead, let all with you
O gentle knight, forget my great offence,
Which I haue purg'd with teares of penitence:
For thoufand liuing eyes with teares could tell,

F 1   That

That from my eies true teares of forrow fell:

Then iudge my caufe with charitable minde,

Who mercie feekes with faith, fhall mercie finde.

This faid, fhe vanifht from before our fight,

I thinke to heauen, and thinke, I thinke aright.

She gone, the poyfon'd ghoaft did feeme with teares

To chide her fate: but loe, there ftraight appeares

The Leiftenants ghoaft.

An

An other in her place, who feem'd to be

When he did liue, fome man of good degree

Mongft men on earth; one of fo folemne looke,

As if true grauity that place had tooke

To dwell vpon; his perfon comely was,

His ftature did the meaner fize furpaffe;

Well fhapt in euery limme, well ftept in yeares,

As here and there appear'd by fome gray haires.

When firft he did appeare, with wofull looke

He view'd the Tower, and his head he fhooke,

As if from thence he did deriue his woe,

Which with a figh he thus begun to fhow.

  O thou fad building, ominous to thofe

Whom with thy fatall walls thou doft inclofe,

For thee, I haplcffe man, as for the ende

Of my defire, did falfly condifcend

Vnto that plot, by others heads begun,

Through which in thee fuch wrong was lately done.

Thou that didft poyfon'd feele thy foes defpight,

See here the ghoaft of that vnhappy Knight,

Which whilome was Leiftenant of this place,

Though now a wretch, thus haltred with difgrace.

The defcription of Sir *Iaruis Ellowis,* the late Leiftenant of the Tower.

F 2   I was

I was, alas, what boots it that I was,
Of good report, and did with credit paſſe
Through euery act of my liues tragedie,
Vpon this world the ſtage of vanity,
Till the laſt ſceane of blood by others plotted,
Concluding ill, my name and credit blotted.
I muſt confeſſe I did conniue at thoſe
That were the miniſters to thy proud foes,
Cloſely imploy'd by them thy life to ſpill
By ſecret poyſon, though againſt my will:
Feare of their greatneſſe, and no hate to thee,
Inforſt my coward conſcience to agree.
When firſt to me this plot they did impart,
O what a tedious combate in my heart,
Vnto my ſoule did feelingly appeare,
T'wixt my ſad conſcience, and a doubtfull feare:
Feare ſaid that if I did reueale the ſame,
Thoſe great ones great in grace, would turne the ſhame
Vpon my head, but conſcience ſaid againe,
That if I did conceale it, murders ſtaine
Would ſpot my ſoule as much for my conſent,
As if at firſt it had bin my intent:

Feare

Feare faid that if the fame I did difclofe,

The countenance of greatnes I fhould lofe,

And be thruft out of office and of place;

But confcience faid that I fhould lofe that grace

And fauour, which my God to me had giuen,

And be perhaps thruft euer out of heauen.

Long thefe two champions did maintaine the field,

Till my weake confcience at the laft did yeild:

O let thofe men that doe condemne my feare

And follie, moft in their remembrance beare,

What certaine danger ftood on either fide

As I fhould paffe, and how I fhould haue di'd

In either way, at leaft with fome great fall

For euer haue been crufht: and thinke withall,

How prone our nature is in feare, to reft

Vpon thofe feeming hopes that promife beft.

I fpeake not this to mitigate my finne,

O no, I wifh my fall may others winne

From the like feare, and that my life may be

A prefident to men of fuch degree,

To whom authoritie doth thinke it fit,

The truft of fuch a function to commit.

Let fuch men to remember ftill be moou'd,

That which by fad experience I haue proou'd;

T'is good to feare great men, but yet 'tis better

Euer to feare God more, fince God is greater:

If Gods good Angel had imprinted this

Into my thoughts, I had not thought amiffe;

Nor I, vnhappie I, fhould haue confented,

But all this mifcheife I had then preuented.

Here fome perhaps will thinke the former race

Of my fad life, t'haue beene debofht and bafe,

Becaufe at laft it had fo bafe an ende;

But for our felues, might modeftie contend

In oppofition, I might iuftly fay,

How many now liue glorious at this day,

Whofe honour greater ftaines doe daily fpot,

Then any which my former life did blot:

Yet thofe my crimes which did my God offend,

For which his finger did point out this ende,

Vnto my life I'le fhew, though to my fhame,

That others as from death may flie the fame.

_{Note.} My Father, from whofe life my breath I drewe,

When ficke vpon his bed he lay, and knewe

That

That at his doore of flefh deaths hand did knocke,

And did perceiue weake nature would vnlocke

To let him in, did with his bleffing giue

This charge to me; that *I* while *I* did liue

Should neuer feeke for office at the Court,

But with that meanes he left my ftate fupport:

With reuerence his will *I* did obey,

Vntill (O that *I* might not tell the day)

*I*n which *I* did with greedy eie affect

That place in this great Tower, without refpect

To my dead Syres beheft; yet fince it was

A touch to confcience, on I would not paffe

Vntill by fome I was refolu'd amiffe,

That as in other things, fo I in this

Which in it felfe was of indifference

And lawfull vnto others, might difpence

With my obedience to my Fathers will,

And that mine owne intent I might fulfill:

Yet one there is (O euer may he be

Belou'd of heau'n for his great loue to me)

Who by the light of truth did fhow the way

Which I fhould goe, but I did not obay:

Ambi-

44   *Sir* Thomas

Ambitious mift did blinde my weaker eyes,
I thought by this preferment I fhould rife;
Yet no defert but gold did gaine me grace.
Mine owne corruption purchaf'd me that place:
For brib'rie in the foule a blemifh makes
Of him that giues, as well as him that takes,
And bribing hands that giue, muft guiltie be
Of their owne want of worth: for who, but hee
That in himfelfe the want of merit findes,
Will be the baude to bafe corrupted mindes?
Ye, that negleft performance of the will
Of your dead parents, thinking it no ill
To difobey their precepts, now in me
The curfe of difobedience ye may fee:
And yee whofe golden fingers, as in fport,
Like lime-twigges catch at offices in Court,
In which obtain'd ye euer after liue
Corrupt in minde, to gaine what ye did giue;
Behold, vntimely deaths difgracefull corde
About this necke, my bribing hands reward.
Before this fuddaine, and vnlookt for fate
Did fall thus heauy on me, when my ftate

Did

Did flourifh among men, to mind I call

An accident of note which then did fall.

Note.

Bewitcht with loue to that too common vice

In this our age, of hazardy and dice,

I loofing once my coine (for few thereby

Haue euer gainers beene) did wifh that I

When I againe did vfe the dice, might come

To die this fhamefull death, which by the doome

Of righteous heau'n, againe I vfing game,

As I had wifht, to mee vnlook't for came.

Vaine gamefters that too commonly vfe

Strange deprecations, when ye doe abufe

Your felues in game, by my fad fall take heede,

And let your word be euer as your deede;

Leaft your hand meete mine in the felfe-fame difh,

For heau'n doth often heare when men doe wifh.

But of no finne had my moft finnefull foule

Beene euer ficke, yet this one finne moft foule,

This act of poyfon, to my houfe a ftaine,

With future times for euer fhall remaine:

The die of blood on murderers hand doth ftay,

No teares, no time, can wipe the fame away;

But

But if true teares of forrow may with you,

(As all true forrowes teares with heauen may doe)

Mooue pittifull regard of my fad fall,

Ye then remembring how I fell withall,

Will out of charity, with leffer blame

Cenfure my fault, when ye fhall heare the fame:

Thus quit by death from doome of Law, and heauen

Out of free mercy hauing me forgiuen,

Let all calumnious tongues their mallice ceafe,

That fo my foule may euer liue in peace:

O let the world abate her fharpned tongue,

And fince I haue done pennance for thy wrong

Thou wronged Knight, what can thy ghoaft now craue?

Grieue thee no more, goe reft thee in thy graue:

Thy foes decline, proud *Gaueston* is downe,

No wanton *Edward* weares our *Englands* crowne.

This faid, he vanifht; and an other ftood

In the fame place, midway aboue the flood,

Whofe

Whoſe ſtrange demeanour with amazement ſtrooke

Vs that beheld him; for with ſtartled looke,

And haire ſtiffe ſtanding, as a man agaſt

He ſtar'd vpon the Knight, from whom in haſt

Into the flood he would haue ſhrunke away,

Had not, I thinke, that fury forſt his ſtay,

Which while he liu'd his guilty ſoule purſu'd,

Till he his owne offence had freely ſhew'd.

G 2 A man

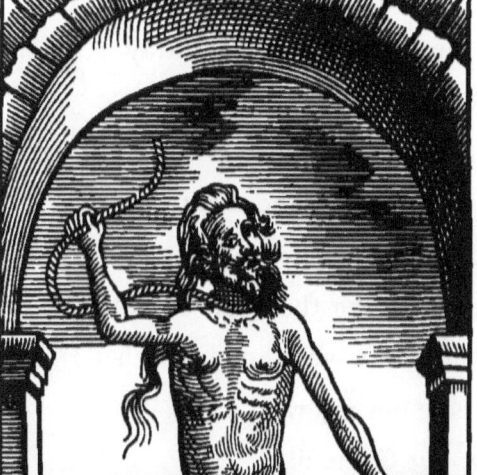

The deſcription of *Franklin.*

Him at the firſt, forſakes that happie way,
Which he ſhould go, and hapleſſe runnes aſtray:
Diſeaſ'd with vanities fantaſticke fittes,
Which ague-like doth vex our Engliſh wittes,
Who thinke at home all homely, and doe plough
Deepe furrowes vpon *Neptunes* waterie browe,
From forreine ſhoares to bring the worſt of bad,
And in exchange leaue there what good they had;
The ſeas I paſt to helpe out my weake skill
In th' *Aromatike* Art, but O the ill,
Which there our ignorant Engliſh oft do finde,
Did firſt corrupt my vncorrupted minde:
O vaine conceit of thoſe, that doe repute
In euery Art the moſt admired fruite
Of any braine; if of domeſticke wit,
But baſe and triuiall, if compar'd to it
Of forreine heads, that onely vs can pleaſe,
And ſuch hath beene our Englands old diſeaſe:
There did I finde, O neuer had I found,
Murthers cloſe way to kill my foe, the ground
Of that deuiſe (thou wronged Knight) whereby
Thou moſt vntimely wert inforſt to die:

There

There was I taught, with vaine words to command
The fpirits from below, who ftill at hand
Will ready bee, as feeming to obay
Thofe foule-blind men, whom they doe moft betray.
Thus hauing, as I thought, my minde enricht
With deepeft knowledge, and with pride bewitcht,
To blow that vaine blaft on the trumpe of fame,
Which through the world I thought might bear my name,
I backe return'd for *England*, there to fhowe
That wondrous skill, which I would feeme to knowe:
There as the Fowler doth with whiftle call
The filly birds, vntill they hap to fall
Into his net; fo did my name each day,
Once blowne abroad, lead fimple fooles away
From helpfull heauen, to feeke aduife in hell,
And there for toyes themfelues and foules to fell:
But in this path long thus I did not tread,
Which downe vnto the houfe of death doth lead,
Before that old flie ferpent did beginne
T' entice me, to that felfe-accufing-finne
Of horrid murther, fhewing me the way
By art of poyfon, clofely to betray

What

What life to death I would, nor did he leaue
Vntill my foule he did fo farre bereaue
Of euery feeling fenfe, that wicked I
Did clofely poyfon her, that vf'd to lie
In mine owne bofome, that fhee beeing dead
Might to me liuing leaue an empty bed:
After this fact, that to my gultie foule
It might not as it was, feeme vgly foule
My fubtile foe did whifper in my eare
Thefe feeming happy newes, how fame did beare
My name vpon her wings, with loud report
Of my ftrange deedes as farre as to the Court;
Where hauing beene employ'd, I with all skill
Apply'd my felfe to pleafe; no damned ill
I did refufe, not making any doubt
While greatneffe wings did compaffe me about.
Forman that cunning Exorcift and I,
Would many times our wicked wits apply
Kind nature in her working to difarme
Of proper ftrength; and by our fpels would charme
Both men and women, making it our fport
And play, to point at them in our report.

Thus

Thus fatted with falſe pleaſure for a while,
Still with good hope of hap, I did beguile
My ſelfe in all imployments, till at laſt
Thy death (thou iniur'd Knight) did with it haſt
My vnexpected fall: I was the man,
That did prepare thoſe poyſons, which began
And ended all thy paine, which I did giue
Vnto that man, who did attendant liue   *Weſton.*
On thee in thy diſtreſſe, who ſince that time
Was he, that firſt did ſuffer for this crime.
O what a ſuddaine change of cheerefull thought
To ſadneſſe, ſelfe-accuſing conſcience brought
After this bloody deed: before all eaſe
Did ſeeme to waite on me; for what could pleaſe
Which I did want? that idol gold, which all
Or moſt men cloſely worſhip, ſeem'd to fall
As thicke vpon me, as the golden ſhower
That fell on *Danae* in the *Dardan* Tower.
Swimming in ſtreames of falſe delight, and prickt
With pride and ſelfe conceit, at heau'n I kickt:
The names of God, and Maker, I did ſleight
As bug-beare words the childiſh world t' affright:

H I   I did

I did impute the fpheares eternall daunce,

And all this all, to nature and to chaunce;

But all men laugh my follies vnto fcorne:

For who fo blinde, will fay being mortall borne,

He hath a reafon, and will yet denie

The fame to this *Vniuerfalitie,*

Of which, alas, he is the leffer part:

As who fhould fay, his feete, his hands, his heart

Might well be wife, and he himfelfe a foole,

Such is the wifedome of th' Atheifticke fchoole.

The eye of heau'n, from whome no heart can hide

The fecret thoughts, my clofe intents efpi'd;

And when I did with moft inuentiue braine,

Deuife to wipe away my confcience ftaine,

And thy fad death moft clofely to conceale,

Heauen forc'd my felfe, my owne felfe to reueale:

The fhadowe of the dead, or fome foule fiend,

Or furie, whom reuenge did iuftly fend

To punifh me for my detefted fin,

With fnakie whippes did fcourge my foule within;

Forbidding me my reft, or day, or night,

Till I had brought mine owne offence to light:

For

For which condemn'd vnto that fhamefull end
Of ftrangling torment, ftill the franticke fiend
Did follow me vnto my liues laft breath;
As was my life before fo was my death.
This faid, he vanifht, and with him that night
The vifion ending, our empoyfoned Knight
Thus fpake: O *England,* O thrife happie land,
Who of all Iles moft gracefully doft ftand
Vpon this earths broad face, like *Venus* fpot
Vpon her cheeke; thou onely garden plot,
Which as an other *Eden* heau'n hath chofe,
In which the tree of life and knowledge growes:
Happie in all, moft happie in this thing,
In hauing fuch a holy, happy King;
A King, whofe faith in armes of proofe doth fight,
'Gainft that feuen-headed beaft, and all his might:
A King, whofe iuftice will at laft not faile,
To giue to each his owne in equall fcale:
A King, whofe loue doue-like with wings of fame,
To all the world doth happy peace proclame:
A King, whofe faith, whofe iuftice, and whofe loue,
Diuine, and more then royall, him doe prooue:
O thou iuft King, how hath thy iuftice fhin'd
Vpon my iniur'd ghoaft, which beeing confi'nd
From hence for euer, neuer had, vnleffe

Thy iuftice had beene great, obtain'd redreffe.
If earneft prayers with heau'n may ought auayle,
And earneft prayers with heau'n doe fieldome fayle;
Let all good men lift vp their hearts with me,
That what I beg, of heau'n may granted be.
If euer heart with wicked thought, fhall aime
To harme thy State, let heau'n reueale the fame:
If euer hand lift vp with violent powre
Shall feeke thy life, heauen cut it off that houre:
If euer eye of treafon lurke about,
Or lie in waite for thee, heau'n put it out:
If heart, hand, eye, abroad or here at home,
Shall plot againft thee, neuer may they come
To their effect, as they haue euer been
So may they be; and let all fay, *Amen.*

    Here my dreame ended, after which a while
Soft flumber did my fenfes fo beguile,
I thought the Tower gate was o're my head,
Vntill I wak't and found my felfe in bed;
From whence arifing, as the wronged Knight
Had giuen in charge, this Vifion I did write.

FINIS.